Puppy Friends™ #5

Max the Muddy Puppy

by Jenny Dale
Illustrated by Frank Rodgers

Aladdin Paperbacks
New York   London   Toronto   Sydney   Singapore

Look for these PUPPY FRIENDS books!

#1 *Gus the Greedy Puppy*
#2 *Lily the Lost Puppy*
#3 *Spot the Sporty Puppy*
#4 *Lenny the Lazy Puppy*

Coming soon

#6 *Billy the Brave Puppy*

First Aladdin Paperbacks edition July 2000

Text copyright © 1999 by Working Partners Limited
Illustrations copyright © 1999 by Frank Rodgers
First published 1999 by Macmillan Children's Books U.K.
Created by Working Partners Limited

Aladdin Paperbacks
An imprint of Simon & Schuster
Children's Publishing Division
1230 Avenue of the Americas
New York, NY 10020

Library of Congress Catalog Card Number: 00-104035
ISBN 0-689-83553-1

Chapter One

"Max, you're filthy!" Simon yelled. "And you smell *horrible!*"

Max, who was sniffing around in the bushes, looked up at Simon, his brown eyes wide. He'd only rolled around in a muddy puddle. What was wrong with that? Max thought he smelled *great!*

Simon took Max's leash out of his coat pocket and grabbed his wet and muddy puppy. "Max, you've got to be the dirtiest puppy in the whole world!" he said, shaking his head. "Come on, let's go home."

Max jumped up eagerly at Simon's legs, wagging his short, stumpy tail furiously. Simon looked down at the muddy pawprints Max had left all over his jeans. "Ma-ax!" he moaned as he clipped the puppy's leash to his collar. "You'll have to take a bath first thing when we get back."

Max's tail stopped wagging. Bath! He hated hearing that word. All the nice smells he'd collected during their walk would be washed away. Simon and his mom always used a shampoo on him

too, which smelled nasty and made Max sneeze. Max hung his head and whined all the way home.

Mrs. Green, Simon's mom, was in the backyard. "Not *again!*" she cried when she saw Max. "He'll have to go straight into the bathtub! I'll go and get it ready."

"I don't want a bath!" Max barked grumpily. But Mrs. Green took no notice and marched off into the house. Max decided that as soon as Simon let him off the leash, he'd run upstairs and hide under one of the beds. They'd never find him there!

"And don't let him off the leash, Simon!" Mrs. Green called as she hurried up to the bathroom. "He'll only hide under one of the beds, and then we'll never get him out!"

"Ugh! Foiled again!" Max sniffed and whined then slumped to the floor, feeling very miserable. It was always the same. Max just couldn't understand it. He was always careful to roll in only the best mud and puddles he could find. But the Greens were never satisfied. They always wanted to wash him!

"Never mind, Max," said Simon, kneeling down to stroke Max's head. "You had to have a bath anyway. We're taking you to the town dog show tomorrow."

Max licked Simon's hand gloomily. He didn't know what a dog show was, but if he had to have a bath to go there, he was pretty sure he wasn't going to like it.

"Simon, you can bring Max up now," called Mrs. Green.

Max refused to budge so Simon had to carry him. Mrs. Green was waiting for them in the bathroom with her sleeves rolled up.

"In you go, Max!" she said, lowering the puppy's sturdy little body into the bathtub. "We'll soon have you nice and clean again!"

Max knew when he was beaten. He sat sulking while Simon splashed warm water over his coat. Then Mrs. Green reached for a big bottle, and unscrewed the lid.

Max's heart sank. "Oh no, not the shampoo!" he woofed. But Mrs. Green took no notice.

"You're going to smell fresh and clean afterwards, Max," Simon told him as his mom poured a drop of shampoo into her hand, then began to rub it briskly into Max's coat.

"Yuck! That smells *horrible!*" Max yelped, sneezing loudly.

"Be quiet, Max!" said Mrs. Green sternly as she and Simon shampooed his shaggy coat.

"You want to look nice for the dog show tomorrow, don't you, Max?" asked Simon.

"I looked nice *before*!" Max woofed back grumpily. Then he yelped again as the shower spray was turned on him and water went up his nose.

"I think you might win a prize tomorrow, Max," said Simon as he lifted his puppy out of the bath and began to dry him with an old towel.

Max didn't know what a prize was, and he didn't care. He was fed up! He'd have to smell like stinky shampoo until Simon took him out for a walk again tomorrow morning. Max thought of all the grubby places he could visit along his favorite muddy lane. He could hardly wait.

"You'll have to keep Max clean tomorrow, Simon," Mrs. Green said. "He mustn't get dirty again before the dog show, so don't let him off the leash."

Max's ears pricked up. This is terrible. Was he going to have to smell like this *all day* tomorrow? Just to go to some silly dog show—whatever *that* was? It wasn't fair!

Chapter Two

"No, Max!" Simon said firmly, the following morning. "I *can't* let you off the leash—you heard what Mom said!"

Max looked up at Simon, pleading with his big brown eyes. He whined and pawed at Simon's leg.

"Well . . ." Simon looked down at his puppy. "Just for a little while, then. But you've got to stay close to me."

Max sat quietly while Simon unclipped his leash. Then he shot off like a rocket. He just couldn't stop himself!

"Max! Max! Come back!" Simon shouted.

Max took no notice as he galloped happily down the lane, through three huge, dirty puddles—splash, splash, splash!—one after the other. The last one was so deep that the water came up to Max's tummy. Max gave himself a delighted shake, then had a quick roll in the dirty water.

"Max, come here!" Simon cried as he ran after the excited puppy. "Mom's going to be *really* mad now!"

Max raced off again, sniffing as he

went. There was a wonderful smell—
one of his favorites—over in a nearby
field. *Cows*.

Max was scared of cows because they
were so big, but cow dirt was fun! He

stuck his head through a gate and looked into the field. To Max's delight, the cows were being led away by the farmer to be milked. He wriggled under the gate and leaped out of reach, just as Simon made a grab for him.

"Max!" Simon yelled as he watched his puppy run across the field. "Keep away from the cow dirt!"

Too late. . . .

Max had already dived into the nearest cow dirt and was rolling around, enjoying himself enormously.

Simon climbed over the gate and dashed over to Max. Holding his nose, Simon grabbed the puppy's collar and pulled him out.

"Max, you *stink*!" Simon groaned. "We're in trouble now!"

🐕   🐕   🐕   🐕   🐕   🐕   🐕

"Simon! I thought I told you to keep him clean!" Mrs. Green gasped when Simon and Max arrived home.

"Sorry, Mom," Simon muttered.

Mrs. Green bent down to scold Max. "Max, you're a very naughty—" She stopped and sniffed, then stepped away. "Is that . . .?"

Simon nodded unhappily. "Yes, he rolled in cow dirt."

Max sat down on the path, feeling pleased with himself. He thought he smelled fantastic!

"He can't come into the house like

that!" Mrs. Green snapped. "And we've got to go shopping now. He'll have to stay out in the backyard."

"But what about the dog show?" Simon asked anxiously.

His mom glanced at her watch. "If we give Max another bath as soon as we get back from shopping, we should get to the show just in time," she said.

Max woofed in disgust. *Another* bath?

Simon shut Max in the backyard, and then he and his mom went out shopping.

Max looked around the yard, feeling very sorry for himself. He brightened up when he noticed a couple of muddy puddles. "Might as well make the most of them before my bath," he woofed.

Max rolled around in puddles for a while, and then dug in the compost heap in the corner of the yard. Then suddenly he smelled something horrible. A soapy, sneezy smell! Shampoo! He wondered where it was coming from and rushed over to the fence to find out. One of the wooden boards was broken at the bottom and Max could push his head through to see down the street.

Missy, the white poodle who lived a few doors away, was trotting toward him with her owner, Mrs. Naylor. Missy's fluffy coat was gleaming white and she was wearing a red bow on top of her head.

Max had never seen a dog wearing a bow before. "Why are you wearing that

thing on your head?" he barked. "You look really silly!"

"It makes me look pretty," Missy snapped. She looked down her nose at Max. "Not like you!"

Max sniffed and sneezed. "You've had a bath, too," he woofed. "Poor you!" He knew that Missy liked to be grubby too. But she didn't often get the chance—Missy's owner was much stricter than Simon.

"Well, I'm going to the dog show, so I have to look nice." Missy stuck her little black nose in the air. "It's usually worth it in the end!" she added rather mysteriously.

"Oh, I'm going to the dog show too!"

Max said. But he hoped that Simon wouldn't want *him* to wear a silly ribbon on his head! "What *is* a dog show, anyway?"

"Don't you know *anything*? Missy yapped. "All the dogs walk up and down and then the judges choose the most beautiful one," she explained.

"Oh." Max preened himself. Surely *he* had a shot at winning!

Missy looked down her nose again. "But to be a winner you have to be clean and smell nice to people. And you don't!" she barked.

Max sniffed. "But I smell great!" he barked back.

"Not to people, you don't," Missy replied.

Mrs. Naylor was becoming impatient and dragged Missy down the street.

"You won't win," Missy barked over her shoulder. "Not like that!"

"We'll see!" Max growled. He had made a decision. He wouldn't wait for Simon and Mrs. Green to come home and give him another nasty bath. No, he'd go to the dog show right now!

Chapter Three

Max had never tried to squeeze through the hole in the fence before. It looked too small. But he was determined to go and check out the dog show.

Max's head went through the hole easily enough. So did his two front legs. But then his tummy got stuck. Max yelped in panic and wriggled hard. Luckily the wood around the hole was rotting away and it broke. Max tumbled out onto the pavement. Phew! He picked himself up and looked down the street.

Missy and Mrs. Naylor were just disappearing around the corner, so Max galloped after them. Keeping out of sight, he followed them until they came to the park. Max often went to the park with Simon on weekends, but today everything looked compeletely different.

There were huge white tents set up on the grass, and lots of booths selling all kinds of doggy things like leashes and toys and baskets and dog food. Crowds of people walked around with their dogs, having fun and eating ice cream cones. Max wagged his tail. This all looked very exciting!

Missy and Mrs. Naylor were making their way over to the biggest tent. Max followed them. A short man and a tall woman were sitting at a table near the entrance. Mrs. Naylor stopped to speak with them, then she and Missy went inside.

Max loped after them but the man at the table reached down and grabbed Max by the collar. "And where do you think you're going?" he asked fiercely.

Max was a bit frightened. He thought he'd better play safe and rolled over onto his back to show the man his cute tummy. It always worked with Mrs. Green.

But the fierce man didn't seem very

impressed. And neither did the woman.

"He's filthy!" she said. "Absolutely filthy!"

"He's got a tag on his collar. Maybe we should call his owner and tell them to come collect him," said the man with a frown. Then he sniffed the air. "What *is* that awful smell?"

The woman came over and sniffed, too. She made a face. "Oh, he smells horrible!"

The man let go of Max's collar very quickly.

Max didn't wait to hear anymore. He escaped, racing off around the side of the tent.

Max snuffled around the back of the tent wondering what to do. Then he began to feel angry. If those silly people wouldn't let him into the dog show, he'd have to find his own way in!

Using his nose, Max managed to lift up the edge of the canvas. He stuck his head in and looked around. There was so much going on that no one noticed him. In the middle of the tent was a big ring. Inside it people and dogs were walking up and down and lots of other people were sitting on benches watching.

Max wriggled under the canvas and into the tent. The dogs in the ring were now lining up and a man was walking up and down, looking them over. Max was amazed to see that all the dogs were just as well washed and brushed as Missy.

Suddenly a delicious smell wafted by. Max sniffed hard. Jerky Treats! He could smell his favorite flavor—beef!

Max decided to go and find where the smell of Jerky Treats was coming from. Perhaps he could grab a few. He trotted off around the tent.

"What *is* that smell?" asked a woman watching the dog show as Max went past.

"I don't know," said the man next to her, looking around. "But it's disgusting!"

As Max walked on, more and more people began to make faces and hold their noses. But Max was too busy sniffing his way to the Jerky Treats.

There they were! There were huge bags of Jerky Treats in a booth in the corner of the tent. As Max watched, a dog and his owner went up to the booth and the nice lady behind the counter gave the dog a Jerky Treat to try.

Max's mouth watered and dribbled onto the grass. He looked up longingly at the plate. It was much too high for him to reach. But he had to get a Jerky Treat somehow.

The saleswoman turned to serve a customer. Then Max noticed an enormous bag of dog biscuits lying on its side on the ground next to the booth. Max wagged his tail. He had an idea. . . .

While the saleswoman was looking the other way, Max scrabbled up onto the bag of dog biscuits, put his front paws against the stall and, straining upward, just managed to grab a Jerky Treat in his mouth. He gave it a sharp tug, and the whole plate of treats flew off the table and onto the grass.

"Aargh!" screamed the saleswoman.

"Look what that dog's done! And what's that *awful* smell?"

Clutching his treat firmly in his mouth, Max beat a hasty retreat. He dived under one of the benches around the ring to eat his snack in peace.

"Mommy, what's that yucky smell?" asked a little girl who was sitting on the bench, watching the dog show.

"I don't know," said her mother with a frown. "Let's move to another seat!"

Max finished his snack in double-quick time and then decided to go and see what the other dogs in the ring were doing. He wriggled out from under the bench and trotted across the tent.

But before he got very far, a hand

suddenly grabbed hold of his collar and held him tightly.

"Can someone *please* tell me who this dog belongs to?" asked a stern voice.

Chapter Four

A grim-faced lady wearing a big, flowery hat was holding Max's collar. Her grip was too tight for him to roll over and try his cute tummy trick on her.

"Who owns this dog?" the woman said in a loud voice. "He shouldn't be wandering around without his leash on!"

Everyone stared at Max disapprov-
ingly. He was beginning to feel very
embarrassed.

"That's the dog that knocked over my
'free sample' plate!" called the woman

from the Jerky Treats booth.

"I think I'd better take you to the lost-and-found tent," said the woman holding his collar.

Max whined and tried to drag himself free. He didn't want to be taken *anywhere*. He wanted to stay and watch the dog show.

"I really don't know what your owner is thinking," the woman went on as she pulled Max away from the ring. Then she sniffed the air. "What *is* that awful smell? Is it you?"

She bent over the puppy to sniff him. As she did so, her big, flowery hat fell off her head and landed right on top of Max. The woman was so surprised, she let go of his collar. Max took off at top speed, still wearing the flowery hat.

"My hat!" the woman shrieked. "That dog's run off with my hat!"

Max couldn't see where he was going. The hat was so big it almost covered him completely. He shook himself hard. The hat flew off his head and Max shot under a bench, out of sight.

Max was panting, but he tried to do it quietly so no one would know he was there. He peeked out from under the bench and saw a boy pick up the hat and give it back to the woman. The hat was now dirty and covered with bits of grass. Max saw the woman sniff it and make a face.

Max was about to bark indignantly, then remembered he was hiding. It was an ugly hat anyway! He slumped down on the grass, wondering what to do now.

Suddenly everyone around the ring started applauding. Max wriggled forward on his tummy to see what was going on.

A line of poodles like Missy was trotting into the ring with their owners. Max's ears pricked up. Missy was there too, with her shiny red bow. Several of the other poodles also wore bows on their heads. All of them were squeaky clean and their fur gleamed. But what a stink all those freshly shampooed dogs made!

Max decided to go into the ring and say hello to Missy. He took a quick look to make sure the woman with the hat wasn't around, then wriggled out of his hiding place.

The poodles in the ring were now sitting quietly beside their owners. Missy and Mrs. Naylor were at the end of the line, and Max raced up to them with a friendly woof.

"Max! What're *you* doing here?" Missy barked, looking shocked.

"I wanted to see what the dog show was like," Max barked back.

"Go away!" Missy yapped. "The judge is about to choose the winner!"

Just then Mrs. Naylor glanced down and saw scruffy, filthy Max sitting next to Missy. She gave a little scream.

"It's me, Max!" Max barked. But he was so dirty Mrs. Naylor didn't recognize him.

"Go away!" she snapped, flapping her hands at Max. "You'll get Missy all dirty!"

"Yes, go away!" Missy barked. "Can't you see everyone's laughing at you?"

Max looked around the ring. All the people watching really were laughing and pointing at him. Suddenly Max felt very small and lonely, sitting there without his owner. He wished that Simon were with him.

The judge was now walking along, inspecting the line of dogs. Max's heart began to thump fast again. It was the hat woman! He had to get out of there before she saw him!

Max dashed across the ring and wriggled his way under the benches. He could hear people talking about him.

"That dog needs a bath—he stinks!"

"Poor little thing! His owner doesn't know how to take care of him."

"People who neglect their dogs like that shouldn't be allowed to have one."

Max barked angrily as he rushed past. "Simon's a great owner!" But no one took any notice.

Max was very fed up. Everyone had laughed at him and now they were saying mean things about Simon, who was the best owner in the world. Max decided gloomily that he definitely didn't like dog shows.

". . . And the first prize goes to Missy and Mrs. Naylor!" boomed the hat woman. "Missy wins a beautiful silver cup. And from our sponsors, a year's supply of Jerky Treats!"

As the judge handed over the silver cup to Mrs. Naylor and Missy, everyone began to applaud. But Max didn't care about a boring old cup. He was thinking about a whole year's supply of Jerky Treats. Maybe he should enter the dog show after all!

Chapter Five

Max ran home from the park as fast as his legs could carry him. He had to get back before Simon and Mrs. Green returned from shopping, or there wouldn't be time for him to have a bath and enter the dog show. Max was so determined to get his paws on those Jerky Treats that he could hardly wait to dive into a tub of warm water and be smothered from head to tail in stinky bubbles. What were a few sneezes if he could win a mountain of Jerky Treats.

Max charged up to the Greens' backyard, and squeezed his way through the hole in the fence. Then he bounded over to the back door and looked up through the kitchen window. There was no sign of Simon and his mom. Max wagged his tail happily. That meant he'd gotten back in time.

A few minutes later Simon and Mrs. Green arrived home. Max began to whine and scratch impatiently at the kitchen door.

"Hello, boy!" said Simon, opening it.

"Don't let him in yet," Mrs. Green began. But it was too late. Max had already dashed past them and was racing up the stairs at top speed.

"Oh no, he's probably gone to hide under one of the beds!" Mrs. Green groaned. "We'll never get him out now!"

Simon and Mrs. Green hurried upstairs after Max. They checked under all the beds but there was no sign of him.

Max woofed. "In here!"

Simon rushed into the bathroom and found Max standing with his front paws on the rim of the bathtub, wagging his tail. "I think Max actually *wants* to have a bath!" Simon said, laughing.

"Quick, let's get him into the tub before he changes his mind!" said Mrs. Green, sounding amazed.

Instead of wriggling about like he usually did, Max sat still while he was being washed. He didn't even move when Simon sprayed him with water. But he couldn't stop himself from sneezing when a bubble popped on his nose.

After Simon had finished rinsing away the suds, he lifted Max out of the bath and rubbed him quickly with the puppy's old towel.

"Use my hairdryer to speed things up, Simon," Mrs. Green suggested.

Max was trying so hard to be good, he didn't even bark at the hairdryer like he usually did. He sat there while the hot air flew over his coat, drying it in no time.

"What do you think, Max?" Simon asked, holding Max up to the bathroom mirror.

Max looked at his reflection and yelped in alarm. His fur, blown dry by the hairdryer, had never been so fluffy! He didn't like it one bit.

Still, looking so silly was for a good cause, Max told himself. It would all be worth it if he won those Jerky Treats. He just hoped he didn't meet any of his doggy friends on the way!

"We must go or we'll be too late to enter Max," said Mrs. Green.

Simon put Max's leash on, and they all hurried off to the dog show.

By the time they arrived at the park, Max was feeling nervous. All the pups he had seen before were much fancier. He didn't remember seeing any dogs like himself at the show. Maybe Simon and Mrs. Green had made a mistake. Maybe everyone in the audience would laugh at him again if he went into the ring with all those fancy pups. . . .

Simon and Mrs. Green took Max over

to the tent and stopped at the table where the fierce man and woman were still guarding the entrance.

"I'm Simon Green, and this is Max," said Simon. "We're entering the Cutest Puppy Competition."

Max's ears pricked up. Cutest puppy? Well, he might not be a fancy pup, but he *was* cute!

"Oh, what a sweetie!" said the woman, bending down to pat Max. Then she frowned. "Funny, he looks familiar. . . ."

"Yes, he does," the man agreed. "I'm sure I've seen him before. . . ."

Feeling alarmed, Max scuttled out of sight behind Simon's legs. If anyone recognized him as the pup that caused all the trouble earlier, he might not be allowed to enter the competition!

Chapter Six

"Will all entrants in the Cutest Puppy Competition please make their way into the ring?"

"That's us, Mom!" Simon said as the announcement came over the loud-speaker.

"Good luck!" said Mrs. Green, giving Max a pat on the head.

Max was nervous as he trotted into the ring next to Simon. He just hoped the woman with the flowery hat didn't see him. He really wanted to win all those tasty Jerky Treats *and* show everyone what a great owner Simon was.

As he and Simon walked around the ring, Max took a look at the other entrants. There were all kinds of puppies—other mutts like Max, as well as fancy pedigrees. Max trotted along with his head held high and his tail wagging hard from side to side. He was determined to be cuter than *any* of the other puppies.

After they'd walked around the ring, all the puppies and their owners lined up, ready to be inspected.

"Here's the judge, Max," Simon
whispered.

Max looked across the ring at the per-
son walking slowly down the line of
puppies, looking them over. His heart
sank. "Oh, no!" he whimpered. It was

the woman with the flowery hat!

"Try to be good, Max," Simon said, patting Max's head. Max gave Simon's hand a quick lick.

But the puppy was shaking a little as the judge came nearer. Would she recognize him?

"What a lovely little puppy! You clearly look after him very well," the judge said to Simon. She smiled down at Max, then made a note on her clipboard. Max allowed his tail to wag, just a little. It looked as if he was going to get away with it! "Mmm . . ." the judge went on. "He seems familiar. Could I have seen him before?" Max's tail stopped wagging.

Simon shook his head. "No," he replied. "This is the first time Max has been to a dog show."

"That's what *you* think," Max woofed quietly.

The judge didn't say anything else. She walked back down the line of puppies, making notes and thinking hard. Then she announced with a smile, "The winner in the Cutest Puppy Competition is . . . Max, who's owned by Simon Green!"

"Max! We won!" Simon yelled, swinging the puppy up into his arms as the audience clapped loudly. *"We won!"*

Max barked his head off. They'd done it! He was officially the cutest puppy!

Now, where was his mountain of Jerky Treats?

The judge presented Simon and Max with a small silver cup. "Congratulations," she said. "And, of course, that isn't all you get!"

Here it comes, Max thought, licking his lips.

"You also get a year's supply of Doggy Delight Shampoo!" the judge went on, and the audience clapped again.

Shampoo? Max could hardly believe his ears! *Doggy Delight Shampoo?* Where were his Jerky Treats?

"Aren't you clever, Max?" said a delighted Mrs. Green as Simon rushed

over to her with Max and the silver cup in his arms. "Now we won't have to buy any shampoo for a year!"

"Oh, great!" Max yapped sulkily.

"Mom, can we buy Max some special treats because he won?" Simon asked.

Max's ears pricked up. *That* was more like it!

"Of course we can," Simon's mom agreed.

As they went over to the Jerky Treats booth, lots of people wanted to pat and stroke Max and tell him what a pretty puppy he was. Simon looked very proud and, even though he hadn't won the Jerky Treats, Max began to cheer up. Maybe it wasn't so bad to be clean and smell "nice" if he got so much attention!

"What can I get you?" asked the woman behind the counter.

"We'll have a big bag of Jerky Treats, please," said Simon. "They're Max's favorite!"

"He's a lovely puppy!" said the woman with a smile. Then she frowned. "Funny, he looks familiar. . . ."

"See, Max?" Simon said happily as they walked home from the dog show. "Being clean *isn't* so bad after all, is it?"

But Max wasn't listening. He'd just spotted an *enormous* muddy puddle.